Angry Ant

Story by Craig Harper • Illustrations by his dad (Ron)

The Angry Ant
By Craig Harper

Copyright © Craig Harper, 2012

Printed in Australia in 2012.
ISBN: 978-0-646-57837-8

Layout & Design: Em Hollister
Adam Brooks Group

Once upon a time, there was an Angry Ant.

Once upon a time, there was an Angry Ant. And wherever the Angry Ant went, he took his anger with him. Sometimes he was angry for no reason. Most times, in fact. It was like there was an angry dark cloud hanging over his tiny ant head. Although his life was quite comfortable, with plenty of food, a nice underground apartment, good health, a family who loved him and a good boss (the Queen), the Angry Ant constantly found reasons to be anything but happy.

Most days he was angry at all the flying insects. He was angry at not having wings. "Why must I walk everywhere with these tiny little legs, while they get to fly in the sky?" he often mumbled to himself. "It's totally not fair." If he had a fist, he would have shaken it at all those airborne showoffs. The only time the Angry Ant almost smiled was when one of those pesky flies got caught in a spider's web. "Serves you right," the Angry Ant would say.

Then there was the sun. Boy did the Angry Ant hate the sun. It made him so hot. And it made him angry too. Although he had a cool underground apartment, he was always complaining about how hot it was above ground. He was angry at the sun most days but not surprisingly, the sun didn't really care about the Angry Ant's anger. Every day through summer he got angry and every day the sun was hot.

It didn't occur to him that being angry at the sun was a waste of good energy.

And then there was the early morning traffic in the ant tunnels. And what traffic it was. Millions of ants all coming and going in different directions. It was enough to get the Angry Ant's blood boiling. If he had blood, that is. All that pushing, shoving and bumping; it drove him nuts. Didn't those other silly ants understand how busy and important he was? Clearly, they didn't. No, they were more concerned with "catching up on the news and having a laugh with their friends". Silly ants. The Angry Ant didn't have time to be held up by those chatty slow pokes. He was important. He had things to do. A job to get done.

Of course, the Angry Ant had happy friends who did their best to encourage him out of his bad moods but the more they tried to make him smile, the angrier he became. In some ways, it was like he wanted to be angry. For some strange reason, their happiness and laughter seemed to annoy him. He was of the opinion that they didn't realise how bad things were. Which is why he often called them 'ignor-ants' behind their backs. A name he thought was most clever. If he was given to smiling, he would have smiled.

But he wasn't, so he didn't.

One day, the Angry Ant was hurrying back to his underground apartment with a crumb. It was a fine crumb. An enormous crumb. A much-bigger-than-him crumb. Even though the Angry Ant already had enough crumbs to last a year, he always wanted more. "You can never have too many crumbs," he would tell his kids. To be honest, his kids would have preferred fewer crumbs in the store room and more play time with their dad. But sadly, their dad didn't really notice.

By the way, did you know that ants can carry twenty times their own bodyweight? If you didn't, now you do.

Anyway (back to the story), the Angry Ant, who was almost hidden by his giant prized crumb, was hurrying along a tunnel at breakneck speed when he tripped over something and fell flat on his ant face. He went one way and his precious cargo went the other. You can imagine how much angrier this made the Already-Angry Ant. If you can't, I'll tell you.

Very. Very. Very.

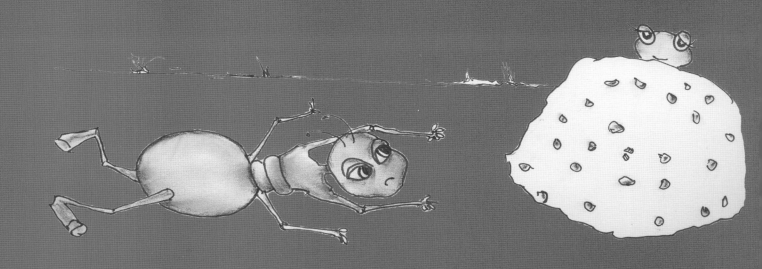

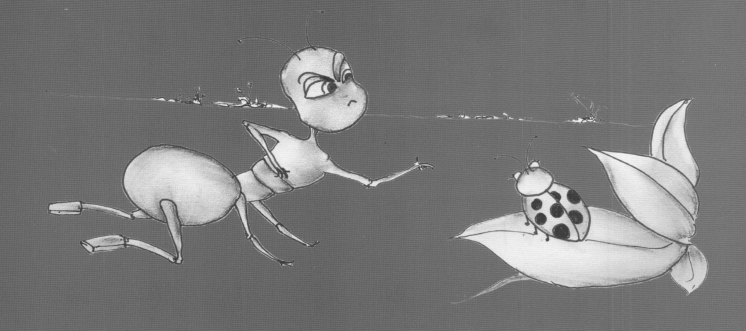

In the blink of an eye (hey, do ants blink?), the Very Angry Ant jumped to his feet. All six of them. He said some not-very-nice words, dusted himself off and peered though the semi-darkness of the underground to see who or what had brought his important mission to a temporary halt. As the dust settled and things became clearer, the Angry Ant began to make out a shape leaning against the wall of the tunnel. The shape began to move. Slowly.

"Ouch," said the shape in a very young voice.

The Angry Ant grew angrier.

"What are you?" barked the Angry Ant.

"I'm a Coccinella Magnifica," came the answer.

"You're a what?"

"You know; a Ladybug. Some call me a Ladybird."

"Why are you in my tunnel, bug?"

"I didn't know it was your tunnel sir," replied the slightly nervous youngster.

"Well, now you do."

"Er, I was on my way to the playground and I got lost exploring."

"Exploring?"

"Yep, exploring. It's fun. Wanna do it with me?" she asked hopefully.

For a moment, the Angry Ant just stared into space. And for another moment, he forgot about his much-bigger-than-him crumb and his very important mission.

"Well?" said the innocent young Ladybug, peering out from behind her big bug eyes.
"Well what?"
"Do you wanna come exploring with me?"
"Don't be ridiculous," snapped the Angry Ant.

The young Ladybug just looked at him.

"Why are you so grumpy?" she asked. "Did something bad happen to you?"

"What do you mean?"

"Well, why are you so nasty to me? I'm just a kid."

For the first time in a very long time, the Angry Ant felt a new emotion; guilt.

"Well, I, er... that is... I...," mumbled the Angry Ant.

"Don't you have people who love you?" enquired the five-year-old (that's five in bug years). "And don't you have friends to laugh with and kids of your own to play with?"

Such smart questions for a five-year-old.

The Angry Ant was feeling awkward and decided to take charge of the situation. As he always did.

"Where are your parents?" he asked sternly.

The young Ladybug just stared at the Angry Ant with tears in her big bug eyes. She blinked and, as she did, her tears fell to the floor of the tunnel.

"They were eaten by a big frog," she sobbed.

The Angry Ant was speechless. And embarrassed. He felt a knot in his ant stomach. He opened his big stupid mouth to say something but no words came out. For once.

Just then, another ant came along and picked up the Angry Ant's giant crumb which had been lying on the ground. Instead of yelling and getting furious, as he normally would, the Angry Ant did nothing. He simply let the stranger take his treasure.

"Mr. Ant, that other ant is stealing your crumb," said the Ladybug between sobs.

"I have enough crumbs already," he replied.

For a moment, everything was quiet. And still.

All of a sudden, the crumb didn't really matter. Right there in the tunnel, something happened deep inside the Angry Ant. He stopped being so angry. And selfish. With no warning, the Angry Ant felt tears welling in his eyes; something that hadn't happened for years. Lots of years. The tears were partly because he felt sorry for the Ladybug and partly because he was ashamed of what he had become; a six-legged nasty-pants.

"How did you get so clever at such a young age?" he asked the five-year-old.

The Ladybug blinked away her tears and just looked at him. Her innocent young eyes were like a mirror to the Angry Ant and he didn't like what he saw.

At all.

He decided to do something about it.

"How would you like to meet my kids?" asked the Angry Ant.

"You have kids?" she asked excitedly.

"Five."

"Wow! Can they play chasey with me? And maybe come to the playground?"

"Yes and yes," said the Angry Ant.

With no warning, the Ladybug leaned over and gave the Angry Ant the biggest hug ever. The Angry Ant felt a lump in his ant throat and once again, the tears welled.

So off they went; the Angry Ant and the Ladybug. To have some fun.

A little while later, surrounded by her five new friends (seven if we count the Angry Ant and his wife), the Ladybug was laughing and playing. Just like a kid should. No more tears. Just fun. It didn't matter that she was a Ladybug and the others were Ants. She didn't care. And neither did they. They were just kids doing kid stuff.

The Happy Ant and his wife sat back and watched the fun. After a while, the Happy Ant turned to his wife. She was the best wife ever.

"I'm sorry," he said.
"I know," she said.

He wasn't used to saying sorry. It felt pretty good. It was much easier than he expected.

As they sat there enjoying the moment, a beautiful butterfly flew right past the Happy Ant and his wife. Knowing how jealous he normally was of winged creatures, his wife felt a little nervous. What would he say? What would he do?

"Wow, how beautiful; I've never noticed all those amazing colours before," said the Happy Ant.

His wife smiled.
And shed a tear of her own.